Weirdibeasts

Weird Snowy Day

There are lots of Early Reader stories you might enjoy.

Look at the back of the book or, for a complete list, visit www.orionchildrensbooks.co.uk

Weirdibeasts
Weird Snowy Day

By Alan, Rachel
and Megan Gibbons

Illustrated by
Jane Porter

Orion
Children's Books

ORION CHILDREN'S BOOKS

First published in Great Britain in 2016
by Hodder and Stoughton

1 3 5 7 9 10 8 6 4 2

Text © Alan, Megan and Rachel Gibbons 2016
Illustrations © Jane Porter 2016

The moral rights of the authors and illustrator have been asserted.

A CIP catalogue record for this book
is available from the British Library.

ISBN 978 1 4440 1284 2

Printed and bound in China

The paper and board used in this book are from well-managed forests
and other responsible sources.

Orion Children's Books
An imprint of
Hachette Children's Group
Part of Hodder and Stoughton
Carmelite House
50 Victoria Embankment
London EC4Y 0DZ

An Hachette UK Company
www.hachette.co.uk

www.orionchildrensbooks.co.uk

For Carl and Harley - J.P.

Contents

Chapter One   11

Chapter Two   21

Chapter Three   31

Chapter Four   45

One

Katie Cat saw it first. It was a single white flake falling from the sky.

Now Katie Cat wasn't just any
old cat.

She was half-cat, half-owl.
"Too-wit too-woo,
too-wit too-woo,"
she hooted. "I think it is starting
to snow!"

As more snowflakes drifted to the ground, the Weirdibeasts crowded round the classroom window.

"Mrs Wonkey, Mrs Wonkey," they shouted. "It's snowing."

Now their teacher, Mrs Creature, was half-wolf, half-donkey and did not like being called Mrs Wonkey.

She prowled up to them . . . then her face lit up.

"Calm down, children," she said.
"Let's get our gloves, coats and
hats from outside the . . ."

But before she could say the word
'classroom' all the Weirdibeasts were
wrestling their way to the door.

They ended up in one big heap
of noses and paws, tails and
claws.

Dabby Dog barked,

Tony Pony neighed,

Penny Pig oinked

and Ricky Rabbit, who was a crabbit, clacked his crabby claws.

clack!

Two

At last they untangled themselves
and soon they were pulling on
their boots . . .

but all the wrong ones!

Big hooves went into little wellies.

Little paws waggled about in
big wellies.

Ricky Rabbit's claws snapped
open and his gloves landed on
Dabby Dog's head.
"I can't see," he yapped.

Finally, Mrs Creature managed
to get some order.
"Settle down, children," she said.
"The younger animals are going
to come out with us. You have
to be good."

"Wait for me," trumpeted a little
voice.
"Who's that?" the animals cried,
looking around.

It was Ellie Mouse. She was all-elephant with her trunk and her tusks, but she was only the size of a mouse!

By now the Weirdibeasts were very excited. They were bouncing up and down like jack-in-the-boxes.

Outside, the snow was settling.
It looked like a sparkling white
carpet.

Finally, Mrs Creature turned the key, looked back at the children with raised eyebrows, and opened the door.

The Weirdibeasts burst out into the snowy yard.

Three

Before long, Katie Cat was perching on the branch of a tree pelting Tony Pony with big, fat snowballs. He was stopping them with his wings and spraying Penny Pig with snow.

Ricky Rabbit was trying to roll
up the snow, but his crabby
claws kept crushing them.

"It's not fair!" he howled as all
the animals wiggled and giggled
and threw snowballs at him.

Penny Pig rolled on the ground
waving her trotters and her fluffy
squirrel tail.
"Look, I'm a snow angel."

"No, you're not," Mrs Creature
chuckled. "You're a snow piggle."
Penny Pig fell about laughing.

"I know," Katie Cat cried. "Let's make a Snowbeast."

"Stand very still," Ricky Rabbit said as all the animals crowded round Katie Cat.

"What are you up to now?" Mrs Creature asked.
As the Weirdibeasts parted, there was a perfect Snowbeast.

"That looks just like Katie Cat,"
said Mrs Creature. "How clever
you are, children."

Suddenly, the Snowbeast let out a loud **sneeze**, a **miaow** and a **too-wit too-woo** and little bits of snow flew everywhere!

As Katie Cat shook the snow from her fur and tail and wings, everybody **oinked** and **neighed** and **barked** with laughter. Even Mrs Creature howled at the fun.

"Stop!" Ricky Rabbit shouted.
"Where's Ellie Mouse?"

The animals looked this way.
They looked that way.

But Ellie Mouse was nowhere to be seen.

Four

Nobody moved. The Weirdibeasts were as still as statues.

"Be very careful, children," Mrs
Creature said. "Ellie Mouse is
very tiny. She must be under all
this snow."
The Weirdibeasts tiptoed carefully
round, dusting the snow away.

Ricky Rabbit started to grab the
snow with his claws.
"No!" the others cried. "Not
you. You'll crush her with those
claws!"

Katie Cat perched on the tree for a better view. She looked down at the yard, trying to see some sign of Ellie.

Tony Pony circled round,
watching the white ground for
any sign of a little, grey body.

There was none.

Mrs Creature had an idea. "Stop, children," she said. "If we all listen very carefully, we might just hear a teeny, tiny trumpety-trump."

All the Weirdibeasts stood very still. Not one wing twitched. Not one feather fluttered. Not one whisker waggled.

Still, there was no sight or sound of Ellie Mouse.

"Just a minute," Katie Cat said, her owl ears pricking. "I can hear something."

**squeak
squeak!**

went a voice – a very tiny voice.

bump bump!

went the door – a very tiny bump.

knock knock!

it went – a very tiny knock.

"I can hear it too," Ricky Rabbit said.
"That's because you've got big ears," said Penny Pig.

They all listened again.

"Let . . . me . . . out," came the voice.

"Let . . . me . . . out!" it came again.

Then, ever so loudly,

"Let me out!"

All the animals rushed across the yard. Opening the door, all they could see was a woolly hat.

"There's something inside,"
said Katie Cat, as a tiny trunk
appeared, lifting the hat up just
enough to show a pair of bright
eyes.

"You shut me in," Ellie
grumbled. "How do you expect
me to reach that handle?"

After that, they all took turns to give her rides in the snow.

It was the best and the weirdest Weirdibeasts' snowy day ever!

What are you going to read next?

Don't miss the other adventures in the **Weirdibeasts** series . . .

Join Katie Cat on her first day at school in **Weird School Day**,

race with the Weirdibeasts in **Weird Sports Day**,

and have some Halloween fun with **Weird Spooky Day**.

For more Early Reader series, including **Monstar**, **Archie and George**, **Mr Monkey**, and **Algy's Amazing Adventures**, visit www.orionchildrensbooks.co.uk

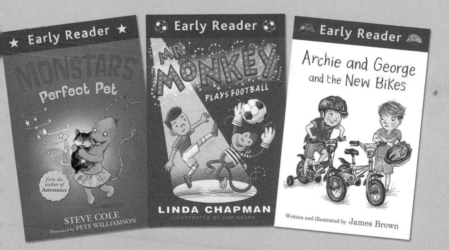